The Talmage Parables

By

JAMES E. TALMAGE

OF THE QUORUM OF THE TWELVE APOSTLES

Book 5 of the James E. Talmage Collection

This book manuscript is considered public domain, and to the best of our knowledge, is complete and accurate in its entirety. The book content reflects the thoughts and opinions of the author, and not necessarily that of the publisher. Minor edits have been added for ease-of-reading and to meet electronic and publication formatting requirements. Latter-day Strengths Publishing makes frequent quality checks of each of our books to ensure that it is formatted properly.

COVER DESIGN: Bryan A. Hunt
IN-HOUSE EDITOR: A. J. Alexander

Latter-day Strengths is an independent publisher of books, eBooks, audiobooks and photography for Latter-day Saints, and is not owned or operated by the Church of Jesus Christ of Latter-day Saints.

Latter-day Strengths Publishing
San Tan Valley, AZ 85143
LatterDayStrengths@gmail.com
Latterdaystrengths.com
Etsy.com/shop/LatterDayStrengths
Amazon.com/latter-daystrengths

Copyright © 2020 Latter-day Strengths

Originally published in The Improvement Era of the Church of Jesus Christ of Latter-day Saints – January 1914 through November 1914.

All rights reserved. No part of this publication may be reproduced, or stored in a retrieval system, or transmitted in any form or by any means, electronic, mechanical, photocopying, recording, or otherwise, without written permission of the publisher. Printed in the U.S.A.

A special thanks to the Internet Archive (www.archive.org) for assisting in the initial preparation of this manuscript.

We donate a portion of every sale to support full-time missionaries of the Church of Jesus Christ of Latter-day Saints.

The *James E. Talmage* collection

Listed in order of original publication date

Book 1: The Articles of Faith (1899)

Book 2: The Great Apostasy (1909)

Book 3: The House of the Lord (1912)

Book 4: The Story of Mormonism (1914)

Book 5: The Talmage Parables (1914)

Book 6: Jesus the Christ (1915)

Book 7: The Vitality of Mormonism Discourse (1917)

Book 8: The Vitality of Mormonism (1919)

TABLE OF CONTENTS

INTRODUCTION 6

JAMES E. TALMAGE 7

THE TWO LAMPS 10

THE DEFECTIVE BATTERY 14

THE PHOTOGRAPHIC PLATE 20

THE OWL EXPRESS 26

THE MINTED COIN 30

THE UNWISE BEE 35

THE TREASURE VAULT 38

THE STORY OF THE CRYSTAL 41

FURTHER LIGHT AND KNOWLEDGE 49

INTRODUCTION

In 1914, as a member of the Quorum of Twelve Apostles, James E. Talmage wrote and published a series of short stories, or parables, in the monthly publication known as The Improvement Era of the Church of Jesus Christ of Latter-day Saints. This book is a compilation of these eight stories which he published throughout that year.

JAMES E. TALMAGE

Biographical Sketch

James E. Talmage
(1862 - 1933)

Elder Talmage served as an Apostle for the Church of Jesus Christ of Latter-day Saints for 22 years. During his life he wrote multiple books that are widely used by Latter-day Saints to this day, including: Jesus the Christ and The Articles of Faith. Elder Talmage also published a series of parables—stories taken from his personal experience that teach gospel principles.

James Edward Talmage was 13 years old when his family emigrated from their native England and settled in Provo, Utah.

Intelligent and thirsty for knowledge, James was a part-time member of the faculty of the Brigham Young Academy in Provo, Utah, by the time he was 17. He went on to study chemistry and geology at Lehigh University in Pennsylvania and at Johns Hopkins University in Baltimore, Maryland. Membership in many prominent scientific societies gave James Talmage access to important people and publications and helped him combat much of the prejudice faced by Latter-day Saints at the time.

In 1888 he married Mary May Booth. They became the parents of eight children. From 1894 to 1897 he was president of the University of Deseret in Salt Lake City (now the University of Utah). During that time he bought one of the popular new chain-driven bicycles and rode it often. One evening he arrived home an hour late for dinner, bruised, bloodied, and dirty. Near his home was a single-plank bridge across a ditch. Normally, he dismounted and crossed on foot. But this time he felt he could ride across. He kept at it, crash after crash, until he mastered the maneuver.

Elder Talmage was an effective lecturer, and some of his talks and lessons became the basis of some of the books for which he is well-known, including *The Articles of Faith.* Prior to his call to the Quorum of the Twelve Apostles in 1911, the First Presidency had asked him to write a book on the life and ministry of the Savior. Later, a room was set aside in the Salt Lake Temple where Elder Talmage could concentrate on his writing. His 700-page book, *Jesus the Christ,* was published in 1915 and has been reprinted several times since then.

THE TWO LAMPS

Among the material things of the past—things that I treasure for sweet memory's sake and because of pleasant association in bygone days—is a lamp. ...

The lamp of which I speak, the student lamp of my school and college days, was one of the best of its kind. I had bought it with hard-earned savings; it was counted among my most cherished possessions. ...

One summer evening I sat musing studiously and withal restfully in the open air outside the door of the room in which I lodged and studied. A stranger approached. I noticed that he carried a satchel. He was affable and entertaining. I brought another chair from within, and we chatted together till the twilight had deepened into dusk, the dusk into darkness.

Then he said: "You are a student and doubtless have much work to do of nights. What kind of lamp do you use?" And without waiting for a reply, he continued, "I have a superior kind of lamp I should like to show you, a lamp designed and constructed according to the latest achievements of applied science, far surpassing anything heretofore produced as a means of artificial lighting."

I replied with confidence, and I confess, not without some exultation: "My friend, I have a lamp, one that has been tested and proved. It has been to me a companion through many a long night. It is an Argand lamp, and one of the best. I have trimmed and cleaned it today; it is ready for the lighting. Step inside; I will show you my lamp; then you may tell me whether yours can possibly be better."

We entered my study room, and with a feeling which I assume is akin to that of the athlete about to enter a contest with one whom he regards as a pitiably inferior opponent, I put the match to my well-trimmed Argand.

My visitor was voluble in his praise. It was the best lamp of its kind, he said. He averred that he had never seen a lamp in better trim. He turned the wick up and down and pronounced the adjustment perfect. He declared that never before had he realized how satisfactory a student lamp could be.

I liked the man; he seemed to me wise, and he assuredly was ingratiating. "Love me, love my lamp," I thought, mentally paraphrasing a common expression of the period.

"Now," said he, "with your permission I'll light my lamp." He took from his satchel a lamp then known as the "Rochester." It had a chimney which, compared with mine, was as a factory smokestack alongside a house flue. Its hollow wick was wide enough to admit my four fingers. Its light made bright the remotest corner of my room. In its brilliant blaze my own little Argand wick burned a weak, pale yellow. Until that moment of convincing demonstration, I had never known the dim obscurity in which I had lived and labored, studied and struggled.

"I'll buy your lamp," said I; "you need neither explain nor argue further." I took my new acquisition to the laboratory that same night and determined its capacity. It turned at over 48 candlepower—fully four times the intensity of my student lamp.

Two days after purchasing, I met the lamp peddler on the street about noontime. To my inquiry he replied that business was good; the demand for his lamps was greater than the factory supply. "But," said I, "you are not working today?" His rejoinder was a lesson. "Do you think that I would be so foolish as to go around trying to sell lamps in the daytime? Would you have bought one if I had lighted it for you when the sun was shining? I chose the time to show the superiority of my lamp over yours, and you were eager to own the better one I offered, were you not?"

Such is the story. Now consider the application of a part, a very small part, thereof.

"Let your light so shine before men, that they may see your good works, and glorify your Father which is in heaven" [Matt. 5:16].

The man who would sell me a lamp did not disparage mine. He placed his greater light alongside my feebler flame, and I hastened to obtain the better.

The missionary servants of the Church of Jesus Christ today are sent forth, not to assail or ridicule the beliefs of men, but to set before the world a superior light, by which the smoky dimness of the flickering flames of man-made creeds shall be apparent. The work of the Church is constructive, not destructive.

As to the further meaning of the parable, let him that hath eyes and a heart see and understand.

THE DEFECTIVE BATTERY

A Laboratory Incident

In the course of certain laboratory investigations, I had need of a primary electric current of considerable power. My assistant prepared a voltaic battery consisting of a dozen cells of simple type. He followed the usual procedure, but, as I discovered later, gave inadequate attention to the details— those seeming trifles that make or mar perfection.

Each cell consisted of a cylindrical jar, containing an acid liquid in which were immersed a pair of plates, one of carbon, the other of zinc. The cells were connected "in series," so that the strength of the battery was the sum of the power developed by the twelve individual units. The working efficiency, or available and usable strength, was the total force developed less the resistance opposed by the cells themselves. The condition is comparable to that of income in the case of an individual or a company; the gross income includes all receipts, from which must be subtracted all costs, if we would determine the net income or actual profit. Or, by another simile, the condition presented by this battery was like that of a mechanical engine, the available efficiency of which is the total energy developed less the effect of friction and all other losses due to imperfect operation.

I was disappointed in the behavior of the battery; its working efficiency was far below what ought to be developed by twelve such units under normal conditions. A casual inspection showed that the cells were not working alike; some of them exhibited intense activity, and in all such the contained liquid was bubbling like boiling water, owing to the escape of liberated gases. The jar was a scene of fuss and fury; yet from such a cell there flowed a current so feeble as to be detectable only with difficulty. The energy developed within those foaming and fuming cells was practically used up in overcoming their own internal resistance, with no surplus power for outside service. I found some cells to be almost inert — with no observable action within, and from such, of course, no current was given out; these cells were practically dead. Certain others were working quietly, with little visible evidence of action aside from the gentle and regular escape of gas bubbles; nevertheless, from the quiet intensity of these, there issued a current potent to transmit messages from continent to continent beneath thousands of miles of ocean turmoil. By diluting the liquid in some jars and intensifying it in others, by replacing a few poorly amalgamated zincs with better ones, and by other modifying adjustments, I succeeded in restraining the wasteful energy of the abnormally active cells, and in arousing to action the dormant ones. The battery was brought into more harmonious operation — just as the restive members of a twelve-horse team might be quieted to steady action, the unwilling ones stimulated, and both brought into unison with their normal and really serviceable fellows.

However, after all such adjustments had been made, the battery was still unsatisfactory. Its operation was weak, irregular, uncertain, and wholly unsuited to the electrolysis required by the work in progress. At length, having become convinced that the fault was a radical one, that some defect was present which no ordinary patching-up process would remedy, I took the battery apart and subjected each cell to an individual examination. One after another passed the test and proved itself to be in measurably perfect condition, until eight had been thus disposed of; the ninth was seriously at fault. This cell was set aside, and the remaining three were tested; all of these were good. Plainly then, the inefficiency of the battery was chargeable to that one unit, number nine; and this, as I remembered, had been among the worst of the abnormally active cells. The eleven good units were connected up; and from the battery thus assembled there issued a current fairly adequate for my needs, and ample to operate an electric receiver or to fire a blast on the opposite side of the globe.

At the first opportunity of convenience I gave closer attention to the rejected unit. There was little difficulty in determining the true cause of the trouble. The cell was in a state of short-circuit; it had short-circuited itself. Through its unnatural intensity of action, as a result of its foaming and fuming, the acid had destroyed the insulation of some parts; and the current that should have been sent forth for service was wholly used up in destructive corrosion within the jar. The cell had violated the law of right action — it had corrupted itself. In its defective state it was not only worthless as a working unit, an unproductive member in the community of cells, but was worse than worthless in that it interposed an effective resistance in the operation of the other clean and serviceable units.

Do you wish to know what I did with the unclean cell? I did not destroy it, nor throw it aside as beyond all repair; there was a possibility of its restoration to some measure of usefulness. I searched its innermost parts, and with knife and file and rasp removed the corroded incrustment. I baptized it in a cleansing bath, then set it up again and tried it out in practical employ. Gradually it developed energy until it came to work well — almost as well as the other cells. Yet to this day I watch that unit with special care; I do not trust it as fully as I trusted before it had befouled itself.

I have called this little anecdote of the defective battery a parable; the story, however, is one of actual occurrence. To me there is profound suggestiveness in the incidents related. Even as I wrought in the laboratory, while hands and mind were busy in the work that engaged my close attention, the under-current of thought — the inner consciousness — was making comparison and application.

How like unto those voltaic cells are we! There are men who are loud and demonstrative, even offensive in their abnormal activity; like unto madmen in their uncontrol. Yet what do they accomplish in effective labor? Their energy is wholly consumed in overcoming the internal resistance of their defective selves. There are others who do but sleep and dream; they are slothful, dormant, and, as judged by the standard of utility, dead.

And again, there are men who labor so quietly as scarcely to reveal the fact that they are hard at work; in their utmost intensity there is no evidence of fussy demonstration or wasteful activity; yet such is their devoted earnestness that they influence the thoughts and efforts of the race.

How like a sinner was the unclean cell! Its unfitness was the direct effect of internal disorder, self-corruption, such defection as in man we call sin, which is essentially the violation of law. In association with others who are clean, able, and willing, the sinner is as an obstruction to the current; the efficiency of the whole is lessened if not entirely neutralized, by a single defective unit.

If you would have your personal prayers reach the Divine destination to which they are addressed, see to it that they are transmitted by a current of pure sincerity, free from the resistance of unrepented sin. Let those who assemble in the sacred circle of united prayer have a care that each is individually clean, lest the supplication be nullified through the obstruction of an offending member.

For him who will seek with earnest intent, there is yet other and deeper significance in the parable.

THE PHOTOGRAPHIC PLATE

An Episode in Field Work

On many occasions during long years of professional service as a mining geologist I have been called to the witness stand in court, there to testify under the solemn obligation of oath, as to results of my examination of mines and of lands supposed to contain deposits of valuable minerals. A certain investigation of the kind extended through many months and involved the inspection of numerous tracts of land covering parts of three states. The particular question at issue was the true classification of the several areas as coal-bearing lands or otherwise. As is requisite in such work, a record of all-important facts as observed was made in the field; and this record, commonly known as the "field notes," was guarded with care, as it would form the basis of all inferences and deductions relating to the investigation.

In due course, more than a year after the completion of the field work, the case came to trial and I was sworn as one of the witnesses. Under both direct and cross examination, I was closely questioned concerning the geologic structure and surface conditions of each of the specific tracts and parcels of land. I was permitted to consult my field notes, and so to refresh my memory, as the lawyers said; but, as would be more accurately stated, to assist my recollection of what I had observed while on the ground.

Concerning one section on which no positive indication of coal occurrence had been found, I was interrogated at length as to the character of the surface. Was there timber on this particular piece? Had the land any value for grazing purposes? Was the land level or hilly? To my surprise I found myself unable to answer with certainty. The field notes relating to this particular area were apparently incomplete; the record contained no surface description at all; there was no entry as to timber, grass, or water, no mention of hills or flats. Naturally, I was disappointed and somewhat embarrassed, as in all other descriptions my notes had proved satisfactory. Recollection failed to supply the information called for. Try as I would I could not call to mind just what I had observed. Beyond all doubt I had been upon the ground, for the notes described the corner stone of the sectional division, and gave in detail its measurements and the chiseled notches by which it was identified as an official land-mark. When about to acknowledge my utter inability to give the data rightly expected of me, just as I was on the point of confessing my seemingly inexcusable failure in a very important part of my work, I was relieved by finding in the note-book one brief entry, which, up to that moment, had escaped my notice. It read simply "S. 10; No. 7." This meant to me that I had taken a photograph at the place referred to in the notes; and the plate on which I would find answer to the questions was No. 7 of Series 10. I had taken many scores of pictures in the course of the long field examination; and the plates had been stored away in the dark room, undeveloped. I asked the court's indulgence until the morrow, promising that then I would furnish conclusive answers to the pending questions.

That night I went to my dark room, and picked out plate No. 7 from the dozen included in Series 10. As shown by the memorandum slip, about fourteen months had passed since that plate had been placed in the camera. With eager expectancy I laid it in the tray and poured upon it the developing liquid. Then, in the faint ruby light of the dark room, lines and shadows gradually appeared, — shall I say like magic? No; but like true miracle, which, however, in this day of popular photography, is counted no miracle but only an ordinary common-place occurrence. When the developing and fixing processes were completed, I examined the plate in a strong light; and there I saw the stone that marked the section corner; there were cattle and my own riding horse, contentedly munching the rich grass, which grew in abundance among stately pines and bright-hued aspen trees; in the foreground was a rippling stream fed by springs, the position of which was discernible in the middle distance of a gentle upland slope. From the negative so produced a print was made; this was taken into court and was there accepted as a full and satisfactory reply to all the questions that had been left unanswered.

The record laid away with the undeveloped plates showed that No. 7 had been exposed a fiftieth of a second. Think of this and forget not the miracle herein made manifest. That plate had been prepared in darkness except for the feeble and non-actinic glow of the ruby lamp; in darkness it had been packed with others in a light-proof box; in darkness it had been transferred to the plate-holder; in darkness it had been placed in the camera, behind the magical wonder-working lens. The cover slide had been withdrawn, leaving the sensitive plate, still in darkness, within the camera box. And then the lens shutter had opened and for one fiftieth of a second the plate had looked out upon the glorious landscape, after which, the shutter closed; darkness again enveloped it, and in darkness it lay for a year and more.

For what to us is a measure of time inconceivably short, the light of the glorious truth of day had fallen upon the sensitized surface of the plate, and all through the subsequent months of dense darkness it remembered the heavenly vision. No tree, no leaf, no flower, no grass-blade was forgotten. But mark you, only after the plate had been immersed in the chemical mixture to which it was responsive was the picture brought out so that men might see and know the truth to which it so convincingly testified.

Is the incident worth reading, worth thinking about? Though of but little merit as a story, it may be of some worth because of the lessons it suggests. Who of us has not realized valuable after-effects from some experience, which, perchance, was relatively as brief and transitory as the view of the sun-lighted scene upon which the photographic plate looked out?

The impress of great truths, caught ofttimes by a momentary flash of heavenly light, are held in store within the hidden recesses of the mind, forgotten, perhaps, for years. Then at a moment of crucial test or painful trial, in the time of distress and affliction, the active reagent compounded in the laboratory of memory and sensitized by the elixir of inspiration is applied, and the picture of the past is brought to light, attesting the truth in a way that none may gainsay or deny.

Let those who minister among their fellows, as teachers of God's word, despair not because of the seeming failure of their efforts. You, my brethren, who through sacrifice and earnest endeavor are devoting yourselves to the saving of souls, be of good cheer, and yield not to the tempter's insinuation that your labors are in vain. It may be that today, by some encouraging word or unselfish act, by some inspired utterance, the full significance of which may have been unrealized by yourselves, you have opened the lens behind which lay a receptive, truth-seeking soul; and though the glory of Divine truth has lightened up that darkened mind for an instant only, the effect is not lost nor will it be forgotten.

Leave the developing of the picture to the Master, who will bring out its lights and its shadows, its verdure and flowers, in his own time, and by means that are to him surest and best.

THE OWL EXPRESS

During my college days, I was one of a class of students appointed to fieldwork as a part of our prescribed courses in geology—the science that deals with the earth in all of its varied aspects and phases, but more particularly with its component rocks, the structural features they present, the changes they have undergone and are undergoing—the science of worlds.

A certain assignment had kept us in the field many days. We had traversed, examined, and charted miles of lowlands and uplands, valleys and hills, mountain heights and canyon defiles. As the time allotted to the investigation drew near its close, we were overtaken by a violent windstorm, followed by a heavy snow—unseasonable and unexpected, but which, nevertheless, increased in intensity so that we were in danger of being snowbound in the hills. The storm reached its height while we were descending a long and steep mountainside several miles from the little railway station at which we had hoped to take [a] train that night for home. With great effort we reached the station late at night while the storm was yet raging. We were suffering from the intense cold incident to biting wind and driving snow; and, to add to our discomfiture, we learned that the expected train had been stopped by snowdrifts a few miles from the little station at which we waited.

The train for which we so expectantly and hopefully waited was the Owl Express—a fast night train connecting large cities. Its time schedule permitted stops at but few and these the most important stations; but, as we knew, it had to stop at this out-of-the-way post to replenish the water supply of the locomotive.

Long after midnight the train arrived in a terrific whirl of wind and snow. I lingered behind my companions as they hurriedly clambered aboard, for I was attracted by the engineer, who during the brief stop, while his assistant was attending to the water replenishment, bustled about the engine, oiling some parts, adjusting others, and generally overhauling the panting locomotive. I ventured to speak to him, busy though he was. I asked how he felt on such a night—wild, weird, and furious, when the powers of destruction seemed to be let loose, abroad and uncontrolled, when the storm was howling and when danger threatened from every side. I thought of the possibility— the probability even—of snowdrifts or slides on the track, of bridges and high trestles which may have been loosened by the storm, of rock masses dislodged from the mountainside—of these and other possible obstacles. I realized that in the event of accident through obstruction on or disruption of the track, the engineer and the fireman would be the ones most exposed to danger; a violent collision would most likely cost them their lives. All of these thoughts and others I expressed in hasty questioning of the bustling, impatient engineer.

His answer was a lesson not yet forgotten. In effect he said, though in jerky and disjointed sentences: "Look at the engine headlight. Doesn't that light up the track for a hundred yards (90 m) or more? Well, all I try to do is to cover that hundred yards of lighted track. That I can see, and for that distance I know the roadbed is open and safe. And," he added, with what, through the swirl and the dim lamp-lighted darkness of the roaring night, I saw was a humorous smile on his lips and a merry twinkle of his eye, "believe me, I have never been able to drive this old engine of mine—God bless her!—so fast as to outstrip that hundred yards of lighted track. The light of the engine is always ahead of me!"

As he climbed to his place in the cab, I hastened to board the first passenger coach; and as I sank into the cushioned seat, in blissful enjoyment of the warmth and general comfort, offering strong contrast to the wildness of the night without, I thought deeply of the words of the grimy, oil-stained engineer. They were full of faith—the faith that accomplishes great things, the faith that gives courage and determination, the faith that leads to works. What if the engineer had failed, had yielded to fright and fear, had refused to go on because of the threatening dangers? Who knows what work may have been hindered, what great plans may have been nullified, what God-appointed commissions of mercy and relief may have been thwarted had the engineer weakened and quailed?

For a little distance the storm-swept track was lighted up; for that short space the engineer drove on!

We may not know what lies ahead of us in the future years, nor even in the days or hours immediately beyond. But for a few yards, or possibly only a few feet, the track is clear, our duty is plain, our course is illumined. For that short distance, for the next step, lighted by the inspiration of God, go on!

THE MINTED COIN

It was once my privilege to make a visit of inspection to the United States Mint at Philadelphia. This is the largest and best equipped establishment of its kind in the country; and within its walls a large proportion of our national coinage is minted, the output ranging from the bronze penny and the nickel piece to the silver dollar with its fractions, thence to the eagle, its half and its double in gold.

I was one of a small party individually invited by the Director of the Mint, under whose official guidance we were conducted through the several departments. In the section devoted to the coining of gold there was great activity, due to the fact that a targe issue of eagles, or ten-dollar gold-pieces, had been ordered by the Treasury Department, of which the Mint is a bureau. As privileged visitors we were allowed to view the processes at close range from first to last.

We observed the preliminary assay of the gold, and the introduction of the small proportion of base metal to ensure the hardness and fineness required by law; then followed the casting of the molten metal into ingots, the rolling of these into strips or fillets each of the exact thickness prescribed. From the thick ribbons of gold, disks were cut, of the diameter and thickness required for the finished coin, and known as blanks or planchets. Though in weight and fineness as true as any eagles in circulation, they were at this stage but smooth pieces of metal; they lacked the stamp that would make them legal tender in the country.

The process that followed next was to me the most impressive of all. The yellow blanks were fed into the great "striking machine" that held the dies. One by one they were delivered to the lower die or anvil; then the arm holding the upper die descended with noiseless precision; and lo! what a moment before had been but an unmarked disk of metal, was now a stamped coin, bearing the attest of the nation as to its genuineness. The pressure exerted upon the piece between the dies was such as to make the gold flow like a viscous mass; a rigid collar confined it, however, and produced the milled edge, while the circular border of the die gave the slight elevation of the rim which is necessary to retard the wearing away of the stamped surface.

Notwithstanding the tremendous force behind the descending die, the operation seemed so gentle, so speedy, and so quiet, as to suggest only a passing touch; nevertheless, the imprinted piece will never forget the experience of that moment. Only through disfigurement can it belie its authoritative stamp; only through acid corrosion, long continued attrition, or destructive violence, can the impress be obliterated; and by such defacement the piece would fall below the established standard of value, and would cease to pass as a legal medium of exchange. The stamped disks, no longer blank, but to all appearances finished coins, were then weighed on an automatic balance of extreme precision, by which any chance defective piece was thrown out.

As a true coin of the realm the yellow eagle issued from the mint. Wherever it goes it will bear testimony to the official impress it received in that moment of pressure and stress, to the authority it bears as an intrinsic endowment, a commission, an appointment, such as shall be respected throughout the country, and even in other lands, for the credit and the official assurance of the nation are behind the stamp on the coin.

Think of what may be done by virtue of the power possessed by that stamped disk of gold. It may bring food to the famishing, clothing to the needy, professional attendance and skilled nursing to the afflicted; it may help to build a cottage, a mansion, palace, castle, or temple. it may go to pay the way on errands of mercy; it may be made a means of relief and blessing to thousands. With such capacity for good, however, there is correlated a corresponding power for evil. That same gold-piece, because of its official stamp, may buy fuel to feed the flames of lust; it may be bartered for the liquor that corrodes body, mind and soul; it may purchase the bomb that destroys the very structure it once assisted to build; it may pass in exchange for the murderer's weapon, and may even hire the murderer; it may prove a veritable curse to its temporary possessor.

Had it never been touched by the die in the mint, had it not received the stamp that insures it currency, it would be just as truly gold, intrinsically worth the full ten dollars for the metal of which it consists; but it would be of no ready service, since every time it changed hands the receiver would have to weigh it and determine its composition. Such necessity would involve consideration, test, calculation, and withal, hesitation and caution, with possible failure to meet the exigencies of the time.

How like that precious gift of God — the assurance and testimony of the gospel of Christ, how like the bestowal of the gift of the Holy Ghost by the authoritative imposition of hands, how like the divine call and ordination to the Holy Priesthood, is the stamp on the coin! The soul so impressed, so chosen, so ordained, shows by word and act as well as by silent influence, the touch of the finger of God, even though the divine contact has been but momentary. Like unto those who are honorable in purpose and honest in heart, yet who have not yet yielded obedience to the requirements of the saving gospel, are the unstamped blanks, good metal though they be. Their influence is limited, their capacity for service narrowly circumscribed. They await the touch, the impress that shall commission them to testify and minister in the name of the King.

To every sterling piece such as tallies with the law of righteousness, that touch shall come in the present or the hereafter, provided only the piece be ready. But how will the metal receive the imprint? If it be brittle through base alloy, untempered, unannealed and unyielding, it may break under the stress, or even though it hold together it may present but a blurred similitude of the authoritative stamp.

Oh soul! hast thou not yet passed between the dies? Dost thou await the individual impress of divine commission? And is thy lack due to unreadiness? Art thou tempered and annealed to receive the testimony of God's approval?

And thou other soul, bearing the imprint of such testimony, art thou true to the stamp thou bearest? Unlike the inanimate coin, thou hast agency and the ability to choose in what service thou shalt be used. Thou art of divine mintage. Great is thy power. Fail not!

THE UNWISE BEE

Sometimes I find myself under obligations of work requiring quiet and seclusion such as neither my comfortable office nor the cozy study at home insures. My favorite retreat is an upper room in the tower of a large building, well removed from the noise and confusion of the city streets. The room is somewhat difficult of access and relatively secure against human intrusion. Therein I have spent many peaceful and busy hours with books and pen.

I am not always without visitors, however, especially in summertime; for when I sit with windows open, flying insects occasionally find entrance and share the place with me. These self-invited guests are not unwelcome. Many a time I have laid down the pen and, forgetful of my theme, have watched with interest the activities of these winged visitors, with an afterthought that the time so spent had not been wasted, for is it not true that even a butterfly, a beetle, or a bee may be a bearer of lessons to the receptive student?

A wild bee from the neighboring hills once flew into the room, and at intervals during an hour or more I caught the pleasing hum of its flight. The little creature realized that it was a prisoner, yet all its efforts to find the exit through the partly opened casement failed. When ready to close up the room and leave, I threw the window wide and tried at first to guide and then to drive the bee to liberty and safety, knowing well that if left in the room it would die as other insects there entrapped had perished in the dry atmosphere of the enclosure. The more I tried to drive it out, the more determinedly did it oppose and resist my efforts. Its erstwhile peaceful hum developed into an angry roar; its darting flight became hostile and threatening.

Then it caught me off my guard and stung my hand—the hand that would have guided it to freedom. At last it alighted on a pendant attached to the ceiling, beyond my reach of help or injury. The sharp pain of its unkind sting aroused in me rather pity than anger. I knew the inevitable penalty of its mistaken opposition and defiance, and I had to leave the creature to its fate. Three days later I returned to the room and found the dried, lifeless body of the bee on the writing table. It had paid for its stubbornness with its life.

To the bee's shortsightedness and selfish misunderstanding I was a foe, a persistent persecutor, a mortal enemy bent on its destruction; while in truth I was its friend, offering it ransom of the life it had put in forfeit through its own error, striving to redeem it, in spite of itself, from the prison house of death and restore it to the outer air of liberty.

Are we so much wiser than the bee that no analogy lies between its unwise course and our lives? We are prone to contend, sometimes with vehemence and anger, against the adversity which after all may be the manifestation of superior wisdom and loving care, directed against our temporary comfort for our permanent blessing. In the tribulations and sufferings of mortality there is a divine ministry which only the godless soul can wholly fail to discern. To many the loss of wealth has been a boon, a providential means of leading or driving them from the confines of selfish indulgence to the sunshine and the open, where boundless opportunity waits on effort. Disappointment, sorrow, and affliction may be the expression of an all-wise Father's kindness.

Consider the lesson of the unwise bee!

"Trust in the Lord with all thine heart; and lean not unto thine own understanding. In all thy ways acknowledge him, and he shall direct thy paths" (Prov. 3:5–6).

THE TREASURE VAULT

Among the news items of recent date was the report of a burglary, some incidents of which are unusual in the literature of crime. The safety-vault of a wholesale house dealing in jewelry and gems was the object of the attack. From the care and skill with which the two robbers had lain their plans, it was evident that they were adept in their nefarious business.

They contrived to secrete themselves within the building and were locked in when the heavily barred doors were closed for the night. They knew that the great vault of steel and masonry was of the best construction and of the kind guaranteed as burglar-proof; they knew also that it contained treasure of enormous value; and they relied for success on their patience, persistency, and craft, which had been developed through many previous, though lesser, exploits in safe-breaking. Their equipment was complete, comprising of drills, saws, and other tools, tempered to penetrate even the hardened steel of the massive door, through which alone entrance to the vault could be affected. Armed guards were stationed in the corridors of the establishment, and the approaches to the strong room were diligently watched.

Through the long night the thieves labored, drilling and sawing around the lock, whose complicated mechanism could not be manipulated even by one familiar with the combination, before the hour for which the time-control had been set. They had calculated that by persistent work they would have time during the night to break open the safe and secure such of the valuables as they could carry; then they would trust to luck, daring, or force to make their escape. They would not hesitate to kill if they were opposed. Though the difficulties of the undertaking were greater than expected, the skilled criminals succeeded with tools and explosives in reaching the interior of the lock; then they threw back the bolts and forced open the ponderous doors.

What saw they within? Drawers filled with gems, trays of diamonds, rubies, and pearls, think you? Such and more they had confidently expected to find and to secure; but instead they encountered an inner safe, with a door heavier and more resistant than the first, fitted with a mechanical lock of more intricate construction than that at which they had worked so strenuously. The metal of the second door was of such superior quality as to splinter their finely tempered tools; try as they would they could not so much as scratch it.

Their misdirected energy was wasted; frustrated were all their infamous plans.

Like unto one's reputation is the outer door of the treasure-vault; like unto his character is the inner portal. A good name is a strong defense, but though it be assailed and even marred or broken, the soul it guards is safe, provided only the inner character be impregnable.

THE STORY OF THE CRYSTAL

A Parable based on Nature's Laws is to be found within

Do you know what a crystal is? Many of us may have seen the beautiful cubes that form when salt solidifies from the brine; the lustrous octahedrons into which alum shapes itself as the substance separates from a saturated solution; and we may have seen, if so we surely have admired, the rhombohedrons of calcite, occurring in the best condition as Iceland spar, and the clear hexagonal prisms of quartz with their pyramidal terminations, each of three or six faces. All of these, the cubes, the octahedrons, the rhombs, and the prisms are crystals, and the geometric forms named are but a few of the multitudinous shapes that are assumed, under certain favorable conditions, when matter returns to the solid state after solution, fusion, or sublimation.

Most solids possessing definite chemical composition tend toward the crystal state. Thus, in addition to the examples already cited, sucrose or cane sugar, tartaric and citric acids, sodium carbonate or washing soda, and sodium bicarbonate or baking soda, may be named as substances common in the home, each of which readily crystallizes provided the conditions are suitable. Gypsum, which is known to many in its massive state only, as plaster-stone or as alabaster, tends toward, and under favorable conditions will attain, the splendid form and state of selenite, which is crystallized gypsum, and which occurs in the vein-cavities and caverns of the earth as monoclinic prisms and other related shapes. When the prisms are very thin and are closely crowded in parallel position, the resulting mass is the rich and lustrous satin spar. The six-sided prisms of quartz, already referred to as occurring in association with terminal pyramids, are specifically known as rock crystal; and it is interesting to note that in reference to this substance the term "crystal" was originally applied. The name is derived from "krystallos," the Greek word for "ice;" and was given to these colorless transparent prisms of quartz on the false basis of a fanciful theory that they were masses of ice that had been frozen by cold so intense as to render thawing-out impossible.

As in part stated above, there is a very general tendency toward crystallization by such chemical substances, either elements or compounds, as are ordinarily solid. Needless to say, the tendency is not always realized; indeed, only under particular conditions do solids actually attain the crystal state. Yet the tendency is ever operative; and there is something inspiringly grand in the tendency itself, — the effort, as we would say were we speaking of living organisms; and in fact there may always be recognized the great and the grand, the noble, the true and the good, in every uplifting tendency, in every effort toward the purer and the better.

The mud in the puddle is an uninviting mixture; nevertheless the constituent parts thereof, the silica of the sand grains, the calcium carbonate of the ground-up limestone, the more complicated silicates of the clay, each of these tends toward, — may we not say, figuratively at least — yearns toward, the state of symmetry in form and structure that is manifest in the crystal alone. If these substances, the chemical ingredients of the dirty, slushy mud, were free to follow their own drift, free to obey unhindered the laws of their inanimate existence, they would all crystallize; and from the mud would come lustrous prisms of quartz, brilliant rhombs of calcite, crystals of feldspar, pyroxene, or possibly some of the silicate gems.

What are these particular and indispensable conditions under which crystals may form? Broadly speaking they may be summarized thus: a state of molecular freedom, whereby the ultimate particles of the substance are made able to move among themselves.

It is known that the axle of a railway locomotive or car may become in time granular, and in consequence very likely to break under any sudden or unusual strain. When the axle was first fashioned it was of fibrous, not granular texture; but the shaking and the jolting, the bumping and the jarring to which it is subjected in long continued travel may bring the particles into the crystalline state. The metal then consists of distinct grains, each a tiny incipient crystal. The granular or crystalline state and the state of actual crystallization fully attained are well illustrated by a lump of loaf-sugar and a cluster of sugar crystals as seen in rock candy. Reverting to the instance of the car axle, we may say that the metal had availed itself of every little jolt or jar to bring its atoms into crystalline relationship with one another. Then some day we hear of an awful disaster. A train is wrecked; many people are injured or killed; investigation shows a defective axle, one that had become granular through long use. Gaged by the standard of human interest the accident was most deplorable and distressing; viewed from the side of natural law it was but an incident connected with the irrepressible effort of homogeneous solids to attain the crystalline condition.

In a lump of rock-salt the tendency toward crystallization is just as real as in salt suspended in water as brine, but the bonds of solidity, the mysterious force we call cohesion, hinders free movement of the atomic particles, and so prevents the orderly molecular arrangement that is characteristic of the crystal state. Solution is one of the processes by which the molecules of a solid are so freed from cohesion as to be able to move without hindrance; and another process of similar effect is fusion or melting under heat.

There are many substances for which no physical solvents are known; that is to say we are unable to dissolve them without first converting them into compounds that are soluble. To this class belong the metals. There are substances that will dissolve in any of several solvents, and others, for each of which but a single solvent is known. Thus, common salt, alum, and sugar are readily soluble in water; and, from the aqueous solution, crystals of the respective substance may be obtained. Camphor is but sparingly soluble in water but easily so in alcohol; and from the alcoholic solution camphor 'may be made to crystallize. Carbon is soluble in molten iron, and may crystallize out from such solution as graphite or as the diamond, each of which is in composition pure carbon. Silicon goes into solution in molten zinc, and crystallizes therefrom in brilliant needle-like forms.

Through the examples cited, certain facts have been established, — that fusion and solution are conducive to crystal formation by affording to the molecules, or ultimate particles of the melted or dissolved substance, freedom to move; and furthermore, that in order to effect the solution of any substance, be it an element or a compound, the particular solvent suitable thereto must be employed.

Like all other operations in Nature, the crystallizing process arouses the wonder and taxes the understanding of the observant student. There is something seemingly supernatural in the shaping of the cubes of salt in a saturated brine, as also in the formation of crystals through cooling and solidification following fusion. Even the unscientific observer sees that the crystal is a manifestation of order; the molecular arrangement is according to system; the symmetry of the crystal is the result of freedom, the fruition of liberty. Hence we have come to say in simile and metaphor, when our ideas on any given subject have been collated and reduced to order and system, that they are crystallized. The figure is a good one, based as it is on sound analogy. To insure the crystallization of ideas through solution, the solvent chosen must be the right one, however rare or precious; aye, though it be the attar of our sweetest fancies, the distillate from false though most-beloved traditions; and to effect crystallization of thought through fusion, the requisite temperature must be attained whatever the sacrifice or cost in fuel, — though we have to cast into the furnace our fondest superstitions, precious prejudices, and even our very passions of hatred or love.

When a great truth enters one's soul for the first time, the man erroneously calls it a new truth; it may give rise to mental disturbance and possible disruption because it is plainly opposed to the man's earlier conceptions. He has to break down his stubborn traditions, his selfish predilections; with pestle and mortar he must grind them to powder, that thus triturated they may the more readily be dissolved or fused. True faith, genuine hope, trust in God, are solvents of rare efficacy; and prayer is the most potent of all. These will in time bring into solution even the most resisting and rebellious thoughts; or, in the furnace, they will develop such heat of conviction as to reduce to quiescent fusion even the most refractory of false beliefs. In the beaker or the crucible shall form new thoughts, freshly crystallized, lustrous, symmetrical, true.

Away back in the last quarter of the eighteenth century there was an exhibition of crystallization of thought and principle on a colossal scale; therein the nation participated; and at the process as at the result the whole world wondered. From the hot solution of united determination there developed gradually the glorious system of government embodied in the Constitution of the United States. The heat necessary to the process was the fire of battle, the fuel was human flesh; the only effective solvent was rich, red, human blood. Oh! what a scene did the laboratory present! The sickening fumes of powder, the shattering impact of bullet, ball, and shell, the stench of gore; the whole rendered more terrifying by shrieks and moans, cries that seemed to have been ripped out of the heart, some like curses, others like prayers. And the heat, — Oh! the heat! It was beyond all that had been ever conceived in the mind of man as possible to earth. The effect of it all was to dissolve in the blood-filled cauldron, to fuse in the flesh-fed furnace, the faith, the hopes, the desires of the people, as well as their antagonisms, their prejudices and their hates. What came from the melting pot and the cauldron? Forms of symmetry and beauty, which in both outward shape and internal structure showed forth order, system, and an approach to the relatively perfect. The ideas of the nation were crystallized, and there appeared the highest type of national government the world had seen.

Who shall say that from the present death-struggle in Europe, the great world war in which slaughter has set a new record for history, there shall not crystallize out from the blood and the fire, higher conceptions of human rights, and a truer realization of God's purposes with respect to man? There has been no dearth of blood, no lack of heat; nor shall the result fail to show forth the glory of the great Chemist, who guides the reactions in cauldron and crucible, and who shall bring from the gory magna a better realization of the truth that men are brothers and that God is Father over all.

FURTHER LIGHT AND KNOWLEDGE

Please look for the next book of the James E. Talmage series ***JESUS THE CHRIST.***

LATTER-DAY STRENGTHS

www.latterdaystrengths.com

Made in the USA
Monee, IL
13 February 2023